The Plague Cycle

In an unnamed country in Africa, a plague is stalking the population. Medical workers, trying to survive themselves, work ceaselessly to help and console stricken villagers, when into their midst comes a benign mysterious near savior, with wings. Implicitly and without fanfare, these beautifully constructed stories—profound, humane, dark, and yet illuminated by love and belief in humanity—bring us into the heart of the global catastrophes facing our species and our planet today. They grapple with pain and loss, but they also shimmer with miracle.

The linked stories in this excellent collection—Maya Alexandri's first—exist half way between timeless fable and the tensely poetic Hemingway of *In Our Time*. They are both dreamlike and unflinching, painting a picture of a parched landscape modeled on the South Sudan, in the grips of a terrible Ebola-like epidemic. Drawn from the author's personal experience and rendered with an artist's attention to surreal detail, *The Plague Cycle* never fails to fascinate.

I was both transfixed and transported by *The Plague Cycle*. Maya Alexandri's writing is so brutal, so particular, so beautiful, and so true that it is difficult to believe this is a work of fiction.

Maya Alexandri's cycle of linked short stories offers a stark and poetic vision of a worldwide epidemic, as experienced through the lives of aid-workers in a small African camp. As these very human heroes struggle to deal with the complex effects of the devastating plague, readers are privy to to an unflinching depiction of the ravages of disease—both physical and psychological, individual and collective—in a voice that moves between clinical and mythological, personal and societal, in a stunning, fast-paced work that leaves behind a residue of both despair and plain, human hope. This is the kind of meaningful fiction that lingers with you long after the first time you read it.

TIMMY REED, AUTHOR OF *KILL ME NOW*, *IRL*, AND *MIRACULOUS FAUNA*

Maya Alexandri writes with the beauty and magic of a different era. The haunting, moving stories in *The Plague Cycle* are like modern day fairy tales. Alexandri's prose lights up the reader's imagination, illuminating a vivid landscape you will never forget.

JESSICA ANYA BLAU, AUTHOR OF *THE TROUBLE WITH LEXIE* AND *THE WONDERBREAD SUMMER*

Under the shadow of a deadly virus, grave-digging becomes routine and knowledge of one's own identity a luxury. *The Plague Cycle* by Maya Alexandri gives us fully realized characters whose breathtaking resilience could be the subject of medical study. The people in these gorgeous stories do something that is at once Herculean and uniquely human—they generate questions … even when life seems to give them nothing but answers.

THE PLAGUE CYCLE

A collection of linked short stories

MAYA ALEXANDRI

SPUYTEN DUYVIL
New York City

Library of Congress Cataloging-in-Publication Data

Names: Alexandri, Maya, author.
Title: The plague cycle : a collection of linked short stories / Maya Alexandri.
Description: New York City : Spuyten Duyvil, [2018]
Identifiers: LCCN 2017051549 | ISBN 9781947980136 (softcover)
Classification: LCC PS3601.L3584 A6 2018 | DDC 813/.6--dc23
LC record available at https://lccn.loc.gov/2017051549

To Doctor Sheik Humarr Khan (1975-2014)

and Chief Nurse Mbalu Fonnie (d. 2014),

formerly of Sierre Leone's

Kenema Government Hospital,

who died in tireless service,

treating those infected with Ebola virus …

… and to Tayeb Salih (1929-2009),

journalist, novelist,

wise, far-seeing poet of the power of compassion

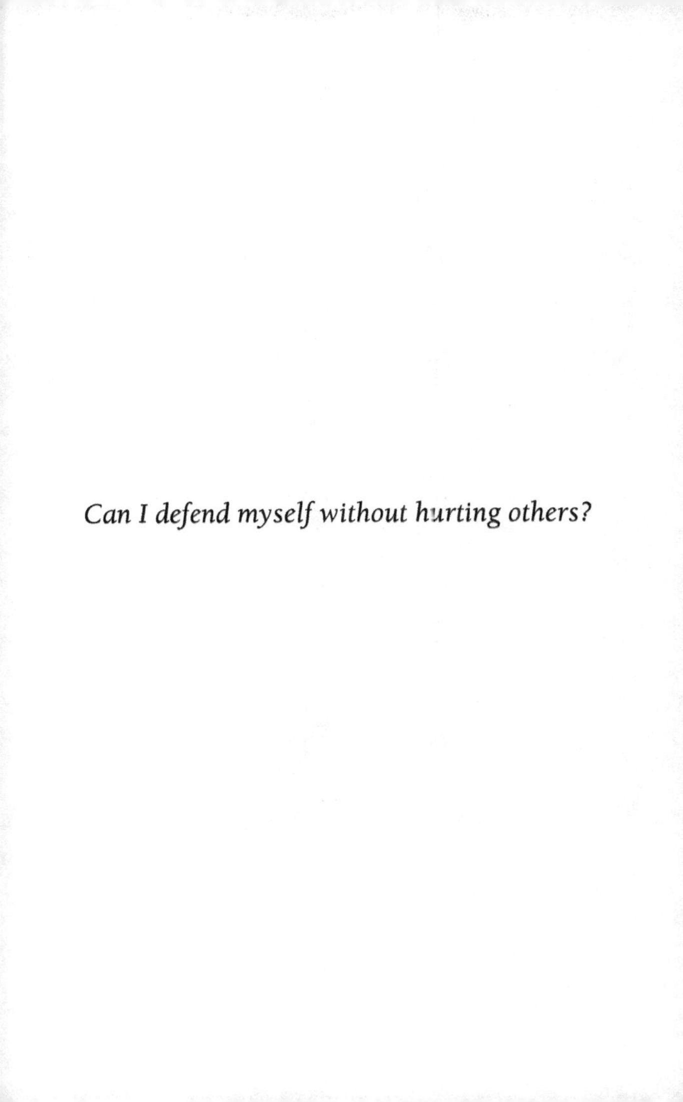

Can I defend myself without hurting others?

The Sudd

The bodies of the seventeen men had been stacked in four piles on two ox carts. The lone survivor had been roped to one of the carts and dragged along, stumbling in the sun, for the duration of the trek to the camp. He was severely dehydrated—sunken eyed—when he was led into the camp director's office. He gave no resistance.

Of course, we gave him water mixed with electrolyte powder. Even though he was an ambusher, we do not take sides. Even against our own enemies.

As instructed, he sipped the electrolyte fluid slowly. In the shade of the office and the gentle currents stirred by the overhead fan, the man revived enough to look fearfully at each of us. We stared back at him with clinical detachment. His wrists and arms were abraded with rope burns.

I arranged my facial features to be as neutral as possible. We all did the same, with varying levels of success. The young medical tech had the least experience and looked angry. The camp director could not prevent his sense of superiority from finding expression on his face.

The ambusher seemed to respond to that assertion of power with an acquiescence of helplessness. He began speaking wildly, incomprehensibly, gesticulating and sputtering, until the director of camp security raised his hand in a gesture calling for a pause. The ambusher's verbiage dribbled away, and he glanced about fearfully again.

"Slow," admonished the director of camp security, not unkindly.

When the ambusher spoke next, he had collected himself. His words were discernible, though like all of us, he undoubtedly spoke at least three languages, and English was not his first.

"*Effendi*, it is true that I and my brethren lay in wait to harm your doctors, but I speak now to warn you for your own protection." He looked at the camp director for approval. We none of us made any change in our facial expression, and after his searching survey found no disapproval, he continued:

"We know each other's habits well," he indicated with his hand, us against him, "and like many times before, last night, we bandits lay in ambush for your caravan. When the Land Rovers came, we saw them halt, as they do sometimes, for some short time, maybe twenty seconds, before driving again, and we know and you know the meaning of that little stop. This time we saw your helicopters make the drops earlier. We saw your doctors, like shadows, running away from the dirt track, across the bush, towards the helicopter drops. We know your strategies of offloading your doctors from the caravan. We have before attacked your caravans of Land Rovers to find them empty of all but drivers and vehicles. We know in the past your doctors have rendez-voused with local guides and helicopter drops of medicines and supplies and made their way on foot under cover of the bush to the camp and evaded our traps. Last night, when we saw the helicopters, we fanned out into the bush to block the doctors' paths, and when they exited the Land Rovers and ran away from the dirt track, they ran towards us."

Now the ambusher stopped. His eyes glazed, and his teeth chattered momentarily. An expression of attention flashed across the camp director's face; he probably thought the man was about to seize. But life returned to the ambusher's eyes, and he continued:

"One of the doctors hit his chest, like this," he motioned, his right hand thudding over his heart, "I saw it," he said, the assertion of bearing witness obviously meaningful for him, but the significance escaped us. "I saw it," he repeated. He began whispering to himself, redirecting his eyes to the floor, and twitching periodically.

"Where are the doctors?" the director of camp security intervened. His voice was sharp, but not mean. "What did you do to them?"

The ambusher snapped his head up abruptly. His eyes were bloodshot now. We all had the same thought: he belonged on our ward. He was sick with the same plague, the recent epidemic that was afflicting all our patients.

"I can only tell you what was done to us."

The statement was surprising. We never considered anything to be done to the ambushers. They were an unfortunate fact of life, like mosquitos and malaria. They are beyond government, beyond justice. Nothing can be done to them. They are not eradicatable. Wherever there travel caravans laden with goods, bandits lie in wait. We knew seventeen of them were dead and stacked in piles on the carts outside, but we considered them to have done that to themselves.

The ambusher was again gripped by teeth chattering. The camp director turned his head to speak to the ward director. Medical treatment was obviously necessary. But the ambusher preempted any order the camp director might have given when he unexpectedly continued:

"It was too large to see in one sight." His voice was clear, but his jaw appeared to be moving without the accord of his mind. His eyes were flickering with confusion, and his hands trembled with strain, as if they were laboring to break loose from tethers. "Its feet were loathsome decay. That must have been the stench, the gut-clenching smell of death. Its feet crawled with maggots and its legs were writhing tendons of snakes. My neck was pulled up. I did not want to look! But my neck was pulled, and my head with it, like I was being hanged, but backwards, hanged upwards, forced to look up to see its terrible groin, an enormous gash of running pustules, sores and open bloody seepage."

His description had a visible effect on us. The young medical tech now looked stricken, and the ward director had covered his mouth with his hand. The camp director seemed torn between deepening professional interest and disgust. The director of camp security, a man who never showed fear, who (I am confident) did not experience fear, wore a facial expression very akin to fear. The ambusher continued:

"Its abdomen was a block of knife blades as dense as river vines and as high as a baobab tree, and its chest and arms an eruption of furious molten rock. I did not want to look, but I was wrenched, hanged, broken into staring up, to its head and its horrifying face! I remember noticing: no screams. There should be screams. We all screamed! Why was it silent?" He looked at each of us now, pleading, as if we might know, might be able to explain.

"Its face was a mountain shard of ice," the ambusher whispered. "Demons live in fire, but nothing can live in ice." He closed his eyes and swallowed thickly. The shaking of his hands escalated. "The mountain crumbled in an avalanche, an avalanche of lifelessness, a wasteland crashing around us, roaring to us. I did not understand. I do not understand its language! It was my bones shaking, the avalanche screaming to my bones." He opened his eyes and stared at the camp director desperately. *"Effendi,"* he beseeched, "my bones understood. It said, 'Let my servants pass.'" He heaved and heaved and began hyperventilating now, gasping, his hands whirlwinding the air around his head. "My brothers fell down dead then, and your doctors ran past into the bush! Don't you see!" he shouted at the uncomprehending expressions that met his revelation: "Your doctors are the servants of Death!"

We none of us spoke, and he ceased to speak. The electric intensity eventually ebbed from him, while indecision slithered over us, and soon a condition of heaviness threatened to freeze us in a tableau, like those pictures Europeans used to paint of the Last Supper.

Then the pharmacy manager knocked on the camp director's door with the announcement, "The doctors are arrived."

When I next saw Dr. Salih, some many years later, she was seated in Dubai International Airport, reading and apparently waiting to board flight 1701 to Monrovia in five minutes. Although I was hurrying to my own gate, and although I was sure she would have no recollection of me, my curiosity overrode my anxieties about missing flights and social impropriety. I had no reason to think I'd see her again; if I was to know, I must ask her now. "Excuse me," I interrupted her and explained who I was, and what I wanted to learn.

She gave me her attention and listened to my request as if my behavior was most natural and proper, as if she'd been expecting me. When I was done speaking, she smiled to herself, perhaps cheered by some memory.

"I told them that he was quite right," she replied. "I told them I was a servant of death, as were they, as are all of us, in that I must go when death summons me."

Unthinkingly, I sat down beside her. I was astonished. I apologized for having misheard her. "I meant, what did you tell the patients after the other doctors gave up and left you with the entire camp? You didn't tell the patients that you were a servant of death."

She nodded pleasantly. "I did."

I argued with her. She didn't remember the facts. Word of the ambusher's warning had leaked from the camp director's office and terrified the patients. They had refused treatment, accused the doctors of being executioners. The other doctors had expressed their sorrow at the folly of witchcraft and had departed. With so many camps of epidemic patients, doctors could not stay where they were not wanted.

Dr. Salih alone had succeeded in persuading the patients to allow her to treat them. She had remained as our camp's sole doctor. And yet, among all the camps that had been organized to quarantine the epidemic patients, ours had been the only one that had suffered no deaths. The only bodies we had buried were those of the seventeen ambushers. And one other.

She continued nodding as I spoke, affirming my summation of the circumstances. "Yes," she agreed, when I finished. "I told them that we are all servants of death, me just as much as them, and that if they wished to begin their service now, I would leave them as they desired me to go. But if they wanted to postpone their service awhile longer, I would stay and do what was possible to coax death to wait."

"And they agreed?" I was flabbergasted.

"Not all of them. Not at first. It was a mother who saved everyone, really. Her baby was probably dying, maybe a day away from dying or so, that's how ill the child was. And she gave me permission to treat her son."

"And he lived."

"Oh yes. He started getting better, noticeably better, in just a few hours, and then everyone else let me treat them."

"But why did she trust you with her infant son?"

Dr. Salih's smile mellowed into a contemplative countenance. "After I spoke, she approached me. No one else would come near, but she walked up to me. She laid the baby in my arms. She surrendered him to me. She said, 'If my son is to die, let him find embrace among the spirits of his ancestors now. Or, if he is to live, let his suffering from this plague end now.' She was, you know, exceptionally brave."

Is brutality good for me?

Tourist in Hades

They had requested that I dig the grave in advance of their arrival.

Per specifications, I dug two meters deep. I did not need concern myself about remaining at least one point five meters above the water table. Here the groundwater lies hundreds of meters below. I fetched plastic body bags for the corpses.

But when the delegation came, it included no dead. The Jeeps carried six Filipino sailors, eleven Chinese stowaways, and a European captain. The captain and two of the sailors each drove one of the three Jeeps. Everyone else lay on canvas stretchers strapped to the vehicles with nautical ropes.

The Jeeps had no roofs, and their occupants were coated with thick red dust. From the port, they had had to drive countless miles over dirt track through the bush. The epidemic ward at the hospital in the port city was no help: it already overflowed with patients dying in queue for treatment. The drive had consumed days.

We assembled at the camp entrance to appraise them. A delegation of foreigners was a special event. We at the camp, of necessity, focus on the needs of the epidemic patients in our care. The demands of our mission isolate us. We did not realize that the plague had spread so far as Hong Kong, that our connection to the rest of the world now included the bond of epidemic. It had not occurred to us that, in caring for those afflicted with this plague, we had something to offer foreigners.

We are careful to greet all newcomers to the camp without judgment. We do not take sides. Neutrality is our creed down to our body language, though we achieve physical neutrality with varying levels of success.

Perhaps by the expression of superiority on his face, and his posture of being an important person, the camp director identified himself. The captain picked him out of our group, called out a respectful greeting from a distance.

After a short discussion, the camp director signaled, and we transferred the patients to triage. The pharmacy manager hurried back to his pills to avoid physical labor. But the stretchers with their cargo were light, and two of us, myself and the triage tech, lifted them without strain.

The patients' symptoms had progressed sufficiently. We could tell at a glance that they, too, were hosts to the same virus whose other victims lay in our ward. We recognized that the men we bore were hemorrhaging. The Chinese men also appeared starved.

The young medical tech brought water to the three drivers, the captain and two sailors. They drank like parched earth soaking up rain.

The captain and his two crewmen allowed the medical tech to escort them to the intake clinic. They, too, required examination. They wore no gloves, facemasks or gowns. They had been exposed to contagion. Within twenty-one days, they too might succumb to the plague.

From triage, in the pre-twilight haze, when the air was thick with red dust and the sounds of birds and insects, I walked to the utility shed to retrieve a roll of tarp and eight bricks. It was well that the expected deaths had not come. A grave delayed of its occupant is an omen of hope. A cover will serve until the time for its use matured.

I carry the tarp and bricks to the grave in two trips. I lay an end of the tarp at the edge of the grave and secure it with three bricks. I unroll the tarp carefully, its water-resistant coating slick on my palms. My foot against the grave's edge tips a shower of clumps of dirt. I look down to reposition my foot and cry out.

A body reaches up to me from the grave.

I fall backwards onto my bum my hands behind me clawing into the dirt. I pedal my feet in front of me. By grace I raise myself and my flailing limbs and flee.

It was the head of security and his assistant who retrieved the captain from the grave and brought him into the office of the camp director. A live patient transferred from the intake clinic to an open grave is a cause for embarrassment. We are professionals. When the occasion for burying a patient arises, it is not because of our incompetence.

The camp director stood when the captain entered the office. His face conveyed a message of sincere concern. "Allow me to apologize —" he began.

"— I am the one who owes the apology," interrupted the captain. He looked around the office, lingering his gaze on me. "I did not wish to be covered with the tarp, that was all," he said quietly. "I meant to frighten no one."

"Our logistics manager perseveres without fear," the camp director assured him quickly, glancing inquiringly at me before falling silent. We no one spoke.

Understanding that the captain, like we all of us, conversed in at least three languages, and that for none was English our first, we all had the same thought: did the captain misuse his English? Or had the captain by his speech implied that he meant to be in the grave? We are aware of the strangeness of the behavior of the Europeans, but we thought it was historical.

The camp director made a gesture to the chair in front of his desk. We all sat down, the captain taking the chair across from the camp director. "A ship disconnects a person from the earth," the captain said with a small smile. "Have you been on a ship?"

The camp director shook his head "no," a constrained motion.

"A container ship, well, that disconnects a person from himself." He laughed. "A container ship is a mast over a vault of boxes, a pulpit over a floating catacomb of coffins, coffins for things. As captain, I hold dominion over a mass of soulless things.

"I thought I wanted that, the company of containers and the efficiency of machines. The absence of souls and the comfort of taking one's place among things that work better than anything else and don't complain because they don't feel."

"If we have failed in our operations," the camp director ventured, "we should like to know the details so that we can improve."

"Failed." The captain pronounced the word as if he had no idea of its meaning.

"How did you come to be in the grave?" the head of security asked politely.

The captain sighed. "There are things that can be explained," he said. "In Hong Kong, a container was loaded onto my ship with fraudulent papers. Its contents were not office furniture, but people. I, who avoid the evils of social interaction, find myself now a trafficker of humans.

"And more. These poor souls penned in the container themselves incubate the virus. This is how we discover them. Four of my crew, co-conspirators with the snakehead, delivered food and removed waste and in the process contracted the virus. When they began to hemorrhage, they confessed. We docked at the nearest port. We drove all our ill to the nearest quarantine facility, which is here. This is what I can explain."

We all of us pondered the word, "explain." We had listened carefully and, if his speech explained something, we did not relate it to our concern. His speech did not suggest that his appearance in the grave had been our error.

"Did you request that the grave to be dug in advance?" the head of security asked.

"Yes." The captain's reply was soft, almost kindly.

A shared reluctance to inquire further took hold of our tongues. We had not erred. Beyond this, what we had learned verged on the intimate. The strangeness of the behavior of this European was not limited to the past. To be taken into his confidence would be a horror.

"I understand that your rapid response test was negative," the camp director addressed the captain, but looked for confirmation to the ward director. The ward director nodded. "The ward director will show you your cot for the night," the camp director stated, "if there is nothing else we can do for you."

I brought two torches to light my work. The sun had set, there was no moon, and the grave remained to be covered. I brought, also, a canvas body bag. A long time it took me to find it in the utility shed. Specifications call for burial of epidemic patients in plastic body bags. The canvas body bags were in our inventory because of a delivery mistake.

Walking from the utility shed to the gravesite, I considered my animal parallel, nocturnal, solitary digger of the red earth: the aardvark. Like me, the aardvark digs to eat. Digs for noble purpose: the aardvark digs shelter for the living; I, a resting place for the dead. Although a burrow is a space below ground with an opening at the surface, it is not an open grave. I am no aardvark.

When I reached the grave site, I saw the

tarp lay partially unrolled and folded over itself, as it had been when I ran off before. I left it as it was.

I shined the beams of the torches into the grave. The captain sat in the corner. When my light illuminated his face, he raised a hand in greeting. I nodded in return.

I felt as if I had been told he would be here.

"May I help you out?" I asked him. My voice was even. I felt no fear, but respect for that which I did not understand.

"Yes," he assented.

I held out my hand, but he made no motion to take it.

"I must ask you to bury me," he said quietly. After a pause, he added, "I am sorry."

"*Effendi* Captain sir," I addressed him, "I cannot do what you ask. Here we do not bury the living."

"My friend, I am not living yet."

I said nothing, made no motion, and

eventually he continued: "I tried. I need your help now. To live."

Among the epidemic patients, strange behavior is not uncommon. I recalled the ward director said that the captain's rapid response test had been negative, but the rapid response test can be wrong. Only twenty-one days quarantine without development of symptoms is a guarantee. The best thing would be to retrieve the ward director. The first thing is to remain neutral.

Seeing no disapproval in my face, the captain continued, "Eighteen months ago, my wife and infant son died in a train mishap. It was many days and many nights that I sat still, unmoving, unspeaking, taking no food or drink, sleeping and waking where I sat, my muscles wasting and the salt collecting on my skin; and after many days and many nights of stillness I discovered that I had descended. Before me was the court of Hades, the Lord of the Underworld presiding over my request behind a veil of water, an irrigation channel dug off the Styx and routed to supply a water feature for the king's throne room in the City of Souls. He bid me go, follow the veil of the Styx from his fountain to wade through the irrigation channel to swim the mighty river across to the living on earth. My wife and child he would send behind me. 'But how will my wife swim when she has to carry our son?' The Lord of the Underworld tolerated my question and bid me go in trust in faith of his promise to send them behind me: 'Your failure of faith will lose them to you forever,' he warned.

"I parted the veil of water with my hands and followed the shower along the reverse of its fall, climbed upwards to the irrigation channel. I walked in this creek of the Styx, its frigid waters swirling around my ankles, every stone on the creek bed polished and painfully cold against my soles.

The waters rose to my shins and knees, to my pelvis and waist, to my sternum and chin, and then the swift waters rushed and my feet were out from under me. My arms cut against the currents howling around and over me. I struggled against the roar of the raging swells, the foam stabbing sharply like icicles against my face. A terrified wail pierced the wall of water noise: my son. His cry caused my body to shake. Submerged in water on the brink of turning solid from cold, my trembling was brought on by my son's cry alone.

"I thrashed now, turned in circles, screaming his name and swallowing the freezing waters when they rushed over my head. Resurfacing, heavy with the water in my stomach and the blood congealing in my veins, I glimpsed behind a veil of water— the Styx and my tears mixed—glimpsed rapidly my dear ones battered by the water's forces. I lunged towards them, my lungs searing with the ice crystals forming along their membranes.

"So it was that I became a captain of a container ship.

"They were lost to me forever, and I stranded mid-river was retrieved by that fearful ferry master, who has tasked me as jester to the gods. I entertain as Charon's parody, ferrying soulless things back and forth, remaining myself between the living and the dead and presiding over goods and machines.

"Oh those souls! Those poor people I unwittingly transported, they are my life-boat out of the river to the shore. They made me stevedore to the living. They brought me here, to you, dear digger! To the precipice of my salvation! Let me know the embrace of the earth, the warmest, fullest, deepest depth of folding into the furrow, and then let me climb out! Let me scratch, crawl, dig, tear my way out, let me free myself from the earth like one born anew and walk away from here alive."

It was now that my neutrality fell away like the dried husk of an ear of maize, and the anger burst present like coals igniting paper. To be asked to be complicit in the suicide of an epidemic patient was a terrible insult. My labor is honest, my courage is great, and my generosity is deep. Myself I put at risk to support the quarantine of epidemic patients. My family, my dear ones, to them I am as across this river he described, I know not where it is, but I am on this opposite side of the shore so that the afflicted may heal, and the unafflicted may live. And this captain thinks me a murderer. I was most angry.

Then—just as the fathomless destructive drive for the source of the Nile routed the rapacious explorers around the Sudd, that endless swamp, that insurmountable obstacle that blocked perception of the Nile river's headwaters and the source of life for the ancients—just so my anger rolled away the stone at the mouth of the cave of my heart, and I found before my eyes this vision:

The captain, hanged from the baobab tree, the rope slung amongst the root-like branches, his broken neck another circuitous, lost route to the bottom of the swamp.

I understood then that it was for me to bury this man, this was my fate. I could bury him alive, or I could bury him dead. But bury this man I would. Compassion is a monster, and tonight I am its servant.

The man must have his story. I found this thought in my head.

I looked at the two torches in my hand, at the canvas bag draped over my arm. I had come prepared, I cannot explain how.

Wordlessly, I squatted at the side of the grave and handed the captain a torch and the canvas body bag. He accepted the torch and the fragile protection of the bag, pulling it over himself and holding the light within, like an embryo in its sac, its vitality sending forth emissary shafts of light.

I placed my own torch on the ground, angled upward to light my work, and picked up my shovel. I counted the shovelfuls of dirt I threw into the grave.

— one, two, three —

I sprinkled the dirt so that much air was layered between the particles, so that the earth would give way when the captain dug up and out of it. The floating particulate of red earth was fragrant of minerals and mosses.

— nine, ten, eleven —

I was careful to arrange the dirt so that it piled most heavily along his sides and legs. I left an airshaft around his face and head, piling the earth around that invisible column. The torch beams shone red through the dancing dirt molecules.

— sixteen, seventeen, eighteen —

When the earth began its tremor, I at first imagined that I was overexperiencing the quaver in my gut. But the muffled growl was unmistakable, and then I saw the slides of dirt rushing into the grave. The trench of the grave was collapsing. When the convulsion ceased, the grave had been reformed as a furrow, each side a sloping indentation of soft, loose dirt.

I sat down beside the furrow, lay the shovel before me. This man's story is very heavy. I would not have burdened him with so much soil. I might wait five minutes, or ten, to know that he is dead. And my own fate.

I counted the minutes by my breath, eighteen breaths to the minute, my eyes closed, the sounds of the night occluded by the intensity of my concentration. It was at thirty-six breaths that the furrow contracted with soft thudding sounds and quivering of dirt.

My eyes flew open. I was witness to the eruption of beams of light, the fingers clawing past the last film of earth into the open night air, the hand gripping the torch so tightly I could see the bones clearly through the skin, the torn canvas bag tatters around his head and shoulders when they emerged, the dirt coating his hair and skin and clothes thick and dark red as blood, his gasping and heaving, his chest cavity and belly straining to expand, to gulp the air deeper and more, the particles of red earth flying and settling, and everywhere the smell of birth.

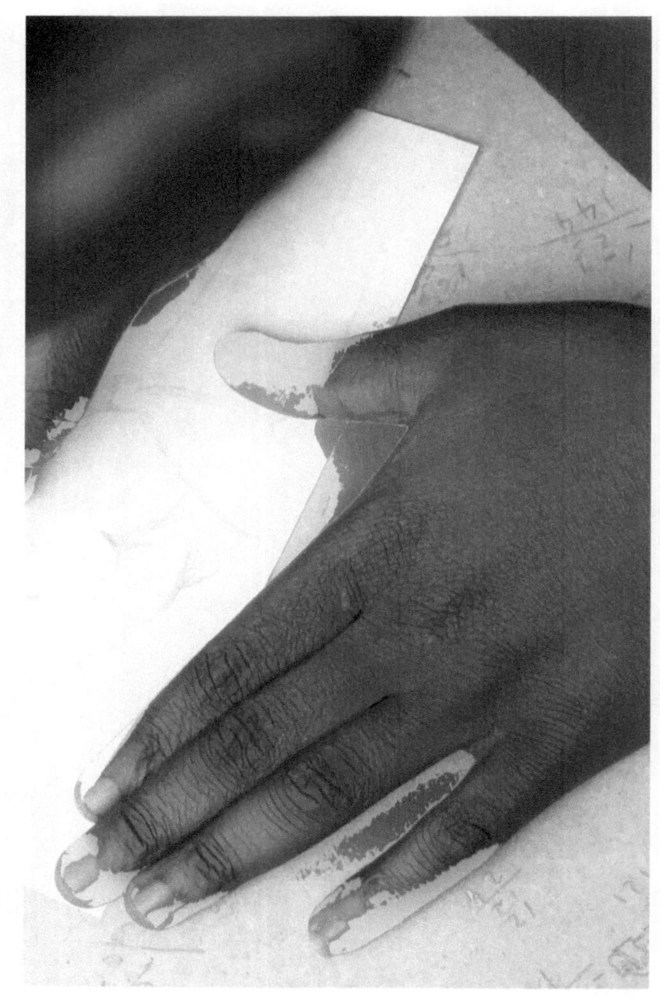

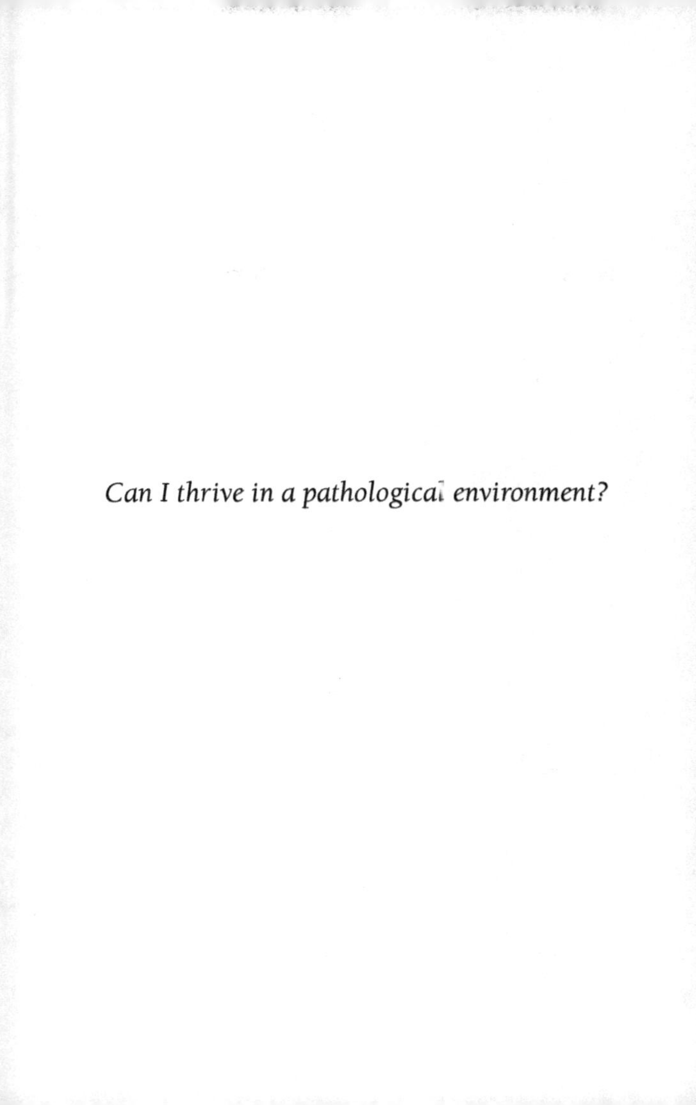

Can I thrive in a pathological environment?

Ghost Limbs

An angel had been sighted on the ward. The reports had come on consecutive nights, from different patients. We do not normally concern ourselves with the patients' visions of the otherworlds. The epidemic patients are often delirious. But one of the patients had endorsed a visitation from the Angel of Death.

We were at the table in the canteen, eating breakfast, when the ward director found us. "He says it has wings," the ward director reported. "Or possibly many arms that move up and down speedily like wings."

The camp director sipped his coffee.

"Is he agitated?" the head of security asked.

"The patient is not agitated," the ward director answered. "He says the experience induced a kind of bliss. The creature hovered over him very close, as if inspecting him, and the patient declares himself now so ready to die that he is almost disappointed to find himself alive."

"Did it do anything besides hover?" the pharmacy manager asked between bites of sorghum porridge. The canteen door slammed. The cook clomped into the canteen, his arms laden with the mangos he had picked.

The ward director hesitated. "He said it emptied his bedpan. It was overflowing."

The camp director made a clipped laugh. "Did it also clean up the spill?"

"Yes," the ward director nodded. "With its wings, or possibly many arms."

"How can it be the Angel of Death if it did not kill him?" the head of security asked, scraping a spoon along the skin of half an avocado and licking the buttery fruit.

The ward director shrugged.

"You have confirmed that it was not just a vision? It did something?" the camp director asked, a crease furrowing his brow. "Was it not the work of your staff that changed the bedpan?"

"No." The ward director looked down and shook his head. "The bedpan was empty when the medical techs came on shift this morning."

The ward director's reply prompted a pause. In the quiet, we all of us had the same thought: we need more staff. We are not in control of the funds available to our quarantine camp. Even at the meager amounts paid for our salaries, we are unable to stretch the budget to accommodate night staff. We tried twenty-four hour shifts, but the days off between shifts were not enough, and we at the camp are also human: we need sleep. Better, it was decided, to have the whole of the staff awake most of the time, then none of the staff fully alert ever.

"There is more." The ward director was nervous. His eyes shifted to the corner of the canteen. "Dressings have been changed. Pain medicine has been administered."

The pharmacy manager looked startled. "Narcotics?"

The ward director nodded. "From the safe. The correct amounts. Intravenously." He took a deep breath. "Charts have been updated. Unsigned," he added.

The camp director placed his coffee cup on the table.

"All this happened last night?" the head of security asked.

"Yes. Over the last two nights, perhaps. We, of course, did not take seriously the report from the first night, but after last night, I made a survey of the status of all the patients and found ...." He stopped, looking puzzled.

"The work of a real angel?" the head of security suggested with a smile.

"I do not know what," the ward director replied.

"Ah, but the patients must be frightened," the head of security reflected. "One patient claims readiness to die, and the rest will panic. You know how rumor affects them. We must calm them. They require an environment suitable to healing."

We all of us nodded. The susceptibility of the epidemic patients to believing the most fantastic stories was well known. They many of them hailed from villages with schools of poor quality. Some had never heard of a virus; the cause of their hemorrhagic fever was a spell cast by a neighbor who is a wizard. Other patients insisted that the government had infected its own population with the virus to steal the funds intended for the villagers' benefit. Our doctor was accused of being a servant of death. With each influx of epidemic patients to quarantine, our ward staff was again charged with complicity in conspiracies to murder patients through the administration of nursing care.

Of course, we understood. Our patients were prey to a virulent plague. It is the nature of humans to witness the hands of gods and devils both in the experience of plague.

"Our camp will be closed if we fail the narcotics audit," the pharmacy manager said flatly.

"The investigation starts today," the camp director declared. He placed both his palms on the table. Amidst the collection of empty juice glasses, porridge bowls, and teacups assembled on the tabletop, his hands appeared powerful.

The head of security and I kept watch in the ward that night. He selected me because I am a survivor of the epidemic. I am immune. The head of security is not immune, but he is a man who experiences no fear. As specifications require of those not immune who enter the ward, the head of security wore gown, gloves, and facemask, and of course he touched no patients. He was protected, but also uncomfortable.

Perhaps for this reason he remained awake while I fell asleep on my watch. I slumbered peacefully in my chair for some hours. It was before dawn when the head of security woke me with a hand on my shoulder. Seated as I was, I was covered with a light blanket. I know not how it came to be there. But I had no opportunity to investigate the blanket's mysterious appearance because the head of security gestured with authority that I should follow. I was still groggy, but I thought I saw a patient getting into bed on our approach.

It was at this patient's bed that we stopped.

Her eyes were closed, but she was not asleep. Sensing us at her bedside, she opened her eyes. The expression on her face betrayed no surprise. She knew why we were standing over her. Though, of course, I did not.

The head of security gestured again. Quietly, so as not to wake the others, she rose from her bed and followed us off the ward. Once outside, the head of security radioed to the camp director.

The patient walked between us to the camp director's office. I noticed that she walked with her arms stiffly held against her sides. Her upper body movement was most unnatural.

We stood outside in the pre-dawn twilight under the setting stars and among the sounds of animals scuffling and a periodic rooster cry. Shortly, the camp director strode into view. He carried under his arm a chart. He wore a facemask, and a gown was slung over his shoulder. He was donning gloves.

"No, no, *Effendi*," the patient addressed

him respectfully. "I am not contagious."

The camp director stopped abruptly and sized up the patient. Her facial expression was sincere, and her posture was sorrowful and apologetic. After a pause, he held up her chart: "Your rapid response test is positive."

"As it is for all who are immune," she said.

He frowned, but peeled off his gloves. "Come in," he said, walking past us and unlocking his office.

The camp director waited for the head of security to take off his gown, facemask, and gloves, and for us all to sit, before he spoke. "Our head of security saw you doing things on the ward," he said. "I think the patients have seen you, too, isn't it correct?"

She nodded.

"You have accessed the narcotics."

She nodded again. "They were in pain. It was prescribed."

The camp director stared hard at her. No sign of arrogance or defiance was apparent. She seemed penitent and also seeking approval. It was a presentation recognizable among village females. They were often beaten.

"And you say you are immune." The camp director paused. The patient's eyes were very large, and trembled. The camp director's voice was concerned, sharp with his confusion, but not unkind, when he asked, "Why are you taking a bed from an epidemic patient who needs one?"

"No, no, *Effendi*," she protested softly. "Yes, perhaps to you it seems so, but no. I am here not doing such bad things as you say. I am a good servant. So much is not my choice it is as if nothing is my choice, but I choose to be a good servant."

Her reply was curious. We understood that the patient, like all of us, spoke at least two languages, and that English was not her first. But her English might be very bad from lack of education. Unfortunately, the patient's village was home to a tribe that spoke a language different from any we spoke.

The head of security attempted to clarify: "Why did you come here if you are not sick?"

"I was sick," she said. "I lay on the woven mats in my family's home hot with fever like desert sand at the highest sun, and my whole family, mother, father, sisters, brothers, aunts and uncles, and their children, all lay beside me, feverish, parched, weak and leaking and wracked with pain, and then bleeding, and then the quarantine officials came and transported us to the camp where they all —"

"— which camp?" the camp director interrupted her.

"Beyt Dakaatra," she answered.

The camp director nodded. "Continue."

"They all died," she said simply.

We all of us inhaled. The death rates from the virus vary at different quarantine camps, as high as ninety per cent in some. Much depends on the care provided to the afflicted. At Beyt Dakaatra, it was known that almost all died.

"I do not remember the camp," she said. "I was in a coma for days, and when I woke up, my family was dead, and I had all these …" her voice faded. We all of us watched her intently. "*Effendi*," she swallowed thickly, "do you believe in witches?"

The camp director looked startled, but answered without hesitation: "No, my child. There is no witchcraft in this world."

"And if it were that I was a witch without intending so, would I be safe here in this camp? If it was the virus that made me the witch?"

The superstition animating this question is common among villagers, and we are careful to withhold judgment from those at the camp. The camp director again answered briskly and without doubt: "Put your mind at ease," he assured her. "We have no witch hunters here."

"I woke up with all these arms," she murmured.

We all of us required a lapse to comprehend her sentence. It was so unexpected. Accepting that we had heard her correctly, we scrutinized her. She had two arms. She wrapped them around her trunk, as if in a desperate hug.

"I see two arms," the head of security said. "The normal number."

"There are nine on each side," she said with absolute resolution and, for a person who speaks with such conviction, it is so. "The staff at Beyt Dakaatra could not see them, either. I begged and begged: 'Saw them off!' Nobody wants a woman with eighteen arms! A monster is such a thing! I pleaded with the doctor there, but he called me crazy, and because my fever broke he sent me away. I walked all the way back to my village, but they did not want me there. To them, all who contract the plague die. Those who return might be ghosts or de-mons."

My heart contracted at her words. I have known the same rejection. It is like the sting of an acid scorpion. It corrodes for a long time.

"And." She looked around her, almost as if evaluating an escape. "And." She looked at the camp director pleadingly, as if he might be able to help her say this diffi-cult thing. He made an expression inviting her speech. It seemed to prompt her. "And the arms demand things. You understand. I have no family now. In my village, I car-ry water. But the arms do not accept that. They are capable. Strong arms. They call for work that is worthy. And I am immune now. I may care for the afflicted without risk. So

I walked to a village where the plague was new. When the quarantine transport came, I played a patient, and it brought me here.

"I sleep at day so I do not trouble the staff, and I wake at night to tend to the patients. This is the service the arms require of me." She addressed the camp director in a piteous voice: "Please do not send me away, like the last camp. Let me serve. Give my bed to an epidemic patient. I will sleep on the floor. It is enough for me."

The patient hung her head, and the camp director looked past her to share a knowing glance with the head of security and me. We are used to the delirium of the epidemic patients. This patient was not sick with the virus, but perhaps a habit of delirium had taken root. Our training is to respond to the person, not the delusion.

The head of security made a start: "Why didn't you apply for a job here? Why did you pretend to be a patient?"

"I cannot read," the patient answered. "I have no education. No training. Before the epidemic, I never left my village. I could never get a job here."

Although females in the villages often cannot read, her answer perhaps had surprised the camp director. He was unusually emphatic in his objections: "But you make notations on medical charts. Administer narcotics correctly intravenously. You change dressings. You are a one-person night staff for the entire ward."

"It is the arms," she insisted. "They can do what I cannot."

At her answer, we all of us felt the grip of frustration. Ignoring her delusion was a poor strategy; against our protocols, she was forcing us to respond to it. And while it is true that we live with the baobab tree in our midst, the "upside down" tree that plants its branches in the soil and stretches its roots to the sky, what succeeds for the tree is no example to emulate: turning the world on its head is not for us.

And, even as that resistance congealed into thought, now it was that I saw unfold, there, where she sat, wings. They were enormous, perhaps a half meter in length, and they were positioned oddly, affixed not to her shoulder blades, as angel wings should be, but growing out from her shoulder joints, from which her arms hung, because—I saw now—the wings were arms, gliding rapidly up and down, making the motion, almost, of wings in flight. The exertion of these many limbs caused her own, two, human arms to unwind from her abdomen and fall open at her sides, while her sternum arched forward and her head tilted back, like she was the Nike of Samothrace embodied. At the sight, I felt an upwelling of joy, as if I had been absorbed into the ecstatic embrace of all my many ten thousand years of ancestors.

An inexplicable demonstration it was, of a piece with her other incredible feats, her tending to the patients with such impossible competency, and of a nature to inspire the kind of trust that is called faith.

The camp director it seems experienced the same revelation. Because what he said next was, "Owing to our budget shortfall, we can pay you only a stipend that will come as a share from my salary—" He held up a hand to stem her protest. "I will arrange it with our accounts manager. And I will make some accommodation with HR. You can begin work today but will attend the next medical tech training."

The camp director then looked at me with a commanding expression that signaled his intention to task me with some responsibility. Without knowing what it was, I nodded my assent.

The camp director turned back to the patient. "And our logistics manager will teach you to read."

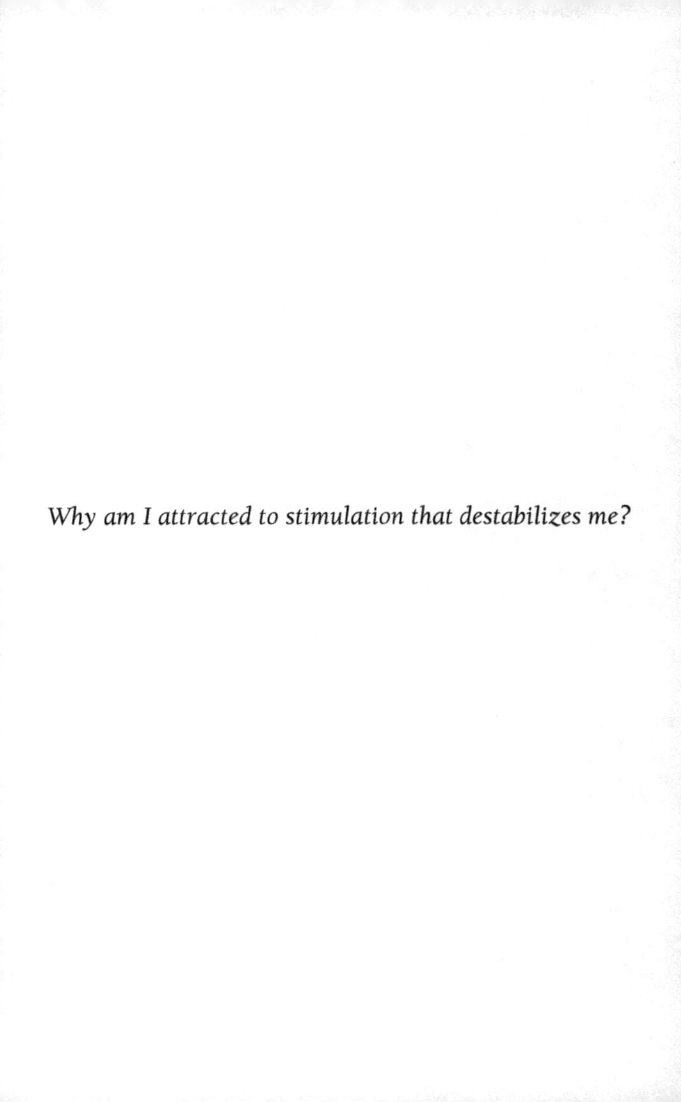

Why am I attracted to stimulation that destabilizes me?

To the Depths

I myself became a gravedigger to avoid the pitfalls of the sex act. It is a good act. But it captured me.

Digging graves was the instruction of an elder from another village. He said: "Return to the earth flesh free of its souls. That is the cure for your ill." This old man I had not met before. What he saw, when he looked, was more than I knew of myself. That is why we need strangers.

We many of us find the body in its shroud disgusting or fearful. To me, it invites tenderness. Life is too hard to be tender to the living. I found that every shovelful of soil upturned to make place for a corpse in the womb of rebirth is a proper subject of tenderness.

We all of us at the camp came to contribute and stay despite hardship for this same reason. We in the camp, the staff and the epidemic patients both, are protected from every harshness, save one. We all of us have food enough and clean water. We have work and rest, and the health of everyone in the camp is tended to. In our mission to care for all those with plague, we have purpose. No harshness do we know, but one: we all of us are beside death. And it focuses the mind.

Today there are no graves to dig, but the borehole needs maintenance. I retrieve the tool box, tarp and air compressor from the utility shed and load them onto the electric cart. I drive through the camp, past the baobab tree that rises beside the patients' ward, to the well.

The well stands within view of the camp entrance: a welcome. A proffer to visitors to sate their thirst.

The hand-pump rising from the circle of the concrete apron looks like a shadow clock. The hour is eight a.m., the heat is at 90 degrees, and the hand-pump casts its shadow to the West and North. It is only a matter of time before we all of us run out of water.

I unfold the tarp on the ground and open the tool box. Using a spanner, I loosen the hand-pump's bolts, nuts and pins, and place these parts one-by-one on the tarp. I remove the hand-pump cover and the counterweighted handle, and I lay them out on the tarp. I am sweating. I inspect the various parts for rust and debris and rub disinfectant on them with a cloth.

In my peripheral vision, I see an epidemic patient at the threshold of the ward. The patient is in street clothes. This patient has recovered well enough to leave the camp.

On some days, a *matatu* comes to pick up passengers. But most *matatu* drivers, like many of our country kin, fear the epidemic patients. Perhaps a person who has recovered from such a plague has been compromised by a demon. We all of us have heard tales of *matatu* drivers abandoning passengers who had been epidemic patients in the bush, or extorting money or visiting violence upon them. Many patients walk home.

I turn to the exposed pump stand. With care, I lift the pump-rod hanger and begin to pull up. This work requires fine calibration. Like a magician pulling scarf upon scarf from the spectator's ear, I draw rod after rod from the ground, and I draw them out gently. The rods are fiberglass-reinforced plastic and threaded together. They are bulky. To bend, break, or damage them risks disaster for lack of replacement parts.

Paying close attention, I fold the threaded rods at their joints and continue to pull up, extracting these limbs from the deep. Holding so many rods is a big exertion. I grab the plunger as it emerges. The pump-rod system in my arms is a heavy weakness. Laying it out on the tarp is like arranging a spindly patient on a bed: almost a skeleton and too limp to move on its own.

"*Effendi*, I ask your pardon."

The voice is soft and melodious. But it is near when I thought myself alone, and so I feel some startle. Looking over my shoulder, I see the patient. She has crossed from the ward to the well. On her head, she wears a bright pink scarf with green embroidery at the border. The effect is to frame her face and make its symmetrical proportions and oval eyes more prominent. "*Begum*, you are welcome," I answer quietly.

She looks down as if stricken with shyness.

I remain kneeling at the edge of the tarp, but I angle my body in her direction. "Are you in need of water for your journey?" I ask. I am prepared to bring her a liter from the staff quarters. The well will not be operational for some hours yet.

She nods. I begin to rise, but sink again to my knees when she says, "Succor. Not water. I need succor. For my journey."

She opens her mouth as if she has not completed her thought, but no sound comes out. I stop and wait on my knees.

"I—" she stammers, after opening and closing her mouth. "You—" Her lips tremble. "Know," she murmurs. "To leave here is to die."

I sit back on my heels and reflect on the ways she is correct. A plague survivor is a person without family. It is the nature of plague to kill the whole household it invades. The survivor is against nature. A person against nature and without family is to be shunned by all. And such a person will die by violence, though perhaps it be the violence of loneliness in exile.

But this epidemic victim will die by the

other sort of violence. She is not of the local tribes. Her facial features look of the North. She is dislocated here. The customs of the Northern people are punitive towards dislocated females. And, of course, she is female.

She watches my thoughts blooming behind my eyes and animating the small muscles of my face, and she is transformed. The shy, stammering, trembling woman relaxes into a column of liquid confidence. "I do not mind to die," she says, "but I like to know the pleasure of sex again before I do." She speaks straightforwardly, without apology. "That was the clarity of my hemorrhagic fever," she adds. She casts her eyes back towards the ward. "When I lay on that bed, like a seeping Venus, red with blood and hot to the touch," she clears her throat, "my thoughts came to focus. Do you," now she pauses to meet my eyes, and finding whatever approval she sought, continues, "know what a clitoris is?"

Her question is not embarrassing to me. I, too, have lain seeping, red with blood and hot to the touch. I, too, recovered. But by virtue of grace, by the grace of good fortune, by the good fortune to have the profession of grave digging at a time when a grave digger is needed at this epidemic quarantine camp, I live in this camp. I do not live in the world. The world will shame this woman before it kills her. So long as she remains in this camp, she will be without shame. And any question is permitted at the precipice of death.

"Yes," I answer her. The uncircumcised women were most beautiful to me always.

She exhales audibly, and I see that she has been holding her breath. "I have all my parts," she says with satisfaction that bleeds a little pride. "I do not mind men, but I prefer women." Her shyness returns and her face flushes. At first, I mistake it for fear of disapproval. I think to assure her that we all of us at the camp make no such judgments. Then I realize that she is recoiling from the possibility of insult to me. "So you understand what I like," she explains.

I have not the words.

I have not even the dead body.

To grab her wrists and thrust her hands into the red earth, manipulating her fingers into claws; to scrape away until a warm crease emerges and to curl, curl her body into the crease—no! To show her my body curled into that crease, to instruct her in covering me, quilting me with the earth— would that teach her? Impart to her the wisdom I gained burying the dead?

That I could take her with me to a morgue! Drag her after me through the cemetery! That I could leave her sentry over stacks of bodies! Task her with upturning dirt for a thousand graves! How else can she understand? How else could I have understood?

I look down and shake my head. "Dear one," I whisper, "I am the addict you recognize. But I no longer use."

She does not argue with me. She continues to stand before me. I do not lift my head. I stay kneeling, gazing on her feet. She wears thin-soled sandals with a leather thong between the first two toes and an ankle strap. I feel the heat of the sun on the back of my head and neck. I decide to rise, to fetch a liter of water for her—water at least she will certainly need, to give her what succor I have to give—when the blare of a *matatu* horn prompts her to turn.

She takes two small steps as she twists her torso to see the *matatu* at the camp gate, the driver barking for passengers to board. She pauses. The driver shouts directly at her now. Like we all of us, insensible to the tender, responsive to the brutal, she follows his order. She crosses from the well to the camp gate and steps from the light of the day into the tinted darkness of the *matutu*. Within it, I cannot see her. And as it drives away, a cloud of agitated red dust obscures even my view of the vehicle's black windows.

The sweat runs from my brow into my eyes, from my neck and armpits down my trunk. My shirt is wet with sweat. The soles of my feet slip on the sweat puddling on my flipflops. My whole body is crying for this woman.

I stand, shade my eyes with my hand, and peer beside the patient's ward at the baobab tree rising defiantly like an inverse taproot out of the ground. Its every root is a well drawing water up from the earth. Because of this tree, we all of us knew the ground on this site bore enough water for our quarantine camp. For the example of this tree, we situated the patient's ward beneath the protective penumbra of its branches, that the patients, too, might draw vitality up through their roots in defiance of their conditions.

I turn and squint down the borehole. It is blackness. In that blackness is some clog, a deposit or incrustation.

Today it is my work to unblock and clean the borehole inner casing. This work is without special meaning. It is work necessary for the inhabitants of this quarantine camp, but it is the job of a gravedigger without a grave to dig. Neither healer nor elder nor shaman, I am merely helpless to do anything but work, and eat, and rest, and die. A one without glory, what victory I know is only over my own urges. I have neither protection nor succor to offer.

And this hopelessness, too, is an urge, a temptation, an addiction.

With this recognition, I see that my work will serve. It is ordinary work, but it will carry a special meaning. Of this work, I will make a ritual. A lay rite that a poor man may do to make of his labour an offering. I will go to the depths for her.

I unfurl the line on the air compressor and lower it through the pump-stand into the borehole, pushing it down, down past the pumping water level. I turn the valve on the line and flip the machine's switch. The line bucks in my hand like a striking snake as the compressed air surges into the borehole. I struggle with the line to push it in farther still. The water shoots up the borehole and I reverse the valve, cutting the injection of compressed air, just at the moment the foaming brown water is poised to erupt from the pump stand. The water sinks away, down the borehole, and I repeat the process again and again: surging and sinking the water piston to power this de-sediment-ing engine.

After eighteen cycles, I open the valve and let the compressed air flow uninterrupted. The brown water rockets up, ejecting the dislodged sediment in a projectile fountain that coats me in a rain of red soil sludge. I push against the line to keep it at its depth, all my strength against this up-rush of defilement, until the geyser runs clean, the aquifer finally liberated from the obstacles to its expression, to its power—the airborne pure water refracting the sunlight like a transient chandelier, an explosion of sunlit diamond drops at its pinnacle, and the waterfall a slapping shower of cooling, stinging sparkles.

I close the valve. The jetting spring subsides. I look at the concrete apron, dark with wet and steaming already in the burgeoning heat. I feel the water beading and evaporating off my arms, the residual minerals and sediment sticking and tight on my skin.

It is only a matter of time before we all of us run out of water. May she know time enough.

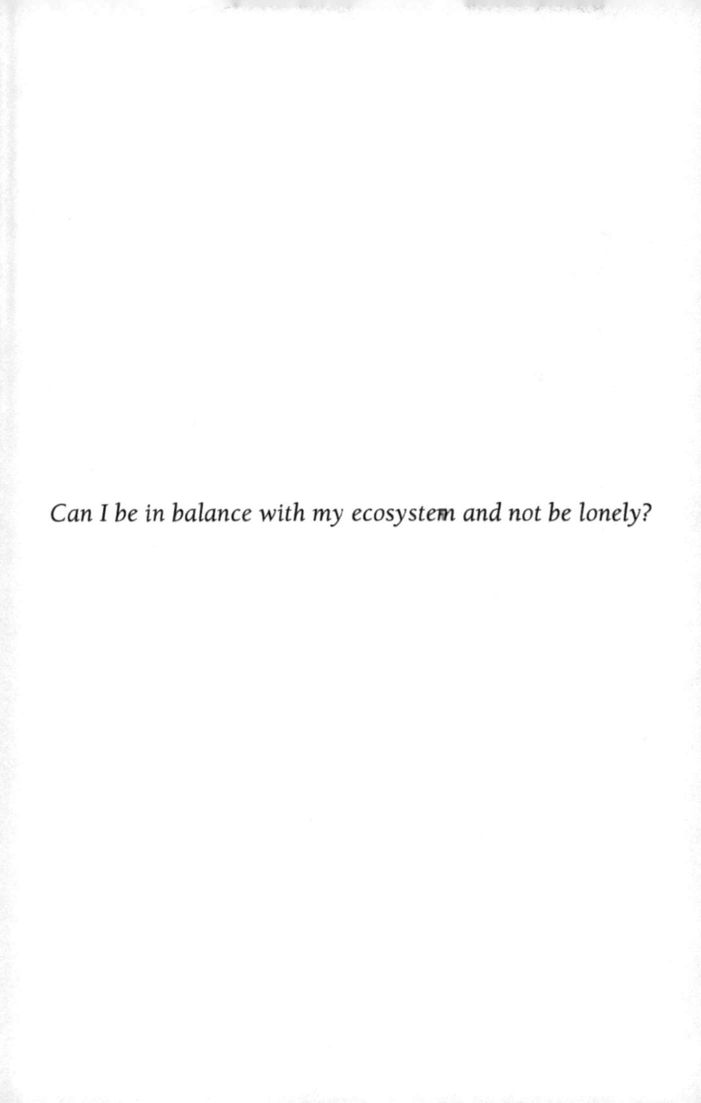

Can I be in balance with my ecosystem and not be lonely?

THE BODY AND THE VIRUS

The day came when we all of us sat down to die. We all of us working at the quarantine camp know that in the European countries, something like this condition is called, "depression." But we all of us were struck together at once, like multi-organ failure in a body. We think the Europeans do not have a name for this group depression.

I myself awoke with the weight. The heart was thick with swamp water, like the Sudd had leaked into my chest. There was no reason to leave the bed. But fear. I was frightened to move, and also frightened to stay in the bed. Then some spasm of dread knocked me to the floor, as if a terrible *afreet* had risen before me, cane in claw to beat me from the bed.

I was not dissatisfied on the floor.

But we all of us were struck at once, so I made my way outside to the area under the overhang and sat on the packed red earth by the door. It was dark still, but the beams from the solar light tower by the ward were sharp.

In the knife light we all of us were apparent under the eaves of our living quarters. Eyes closed, the ward director sat limp like he was asleep, except that his appearance was not peaceful. The pharmacy manager stared vacant into space. Beneath the window, the triage tech was almost unrecognizable, hunched over and shirtless. The head of security, a man who knows no fear, was crying, silently, fat tears glinting runnels along his cheeks. Our camp director was curled in fetal position.

Our dream was this:

In the pathways within for blood and lymph and the spirits of our ancestors, the virus is shaped like a snake twisted around itself and prepared to strike. These pathways are crowded with cells and gasses and molecules jostling and bumping. The snake bites the passing macrophage immune cell. The cell membrane collapses around the snakebite, surrounding it like a balloon, pinching off from the membrane and falling inward into the cytoplasm, the snake fangs hooked into the bubble, the snake-virus breaching the barricade. The macrophage exists to eat invaders, but this snake vomits itself into the cytoplasm: a filament of RNA, a polymerase protein. These hijack the equipment innate to the cell. The macrophage's own ribosomes labor like slaves, manufacturing the virus proteins that assemble countless snake clones. The snake clones rupture out of the macrophage, which has traveled to the liver, gall bladder, pancreas, spleen, and so the snake bites organ after organ, and the cycle continues: breach, vomit, slave, rupture, breach, vomit, slave, rupture.

Wildly, the macrophages unleash their whiplashing cytokines—necrosis factors, inflammatory proteins, interleukins, chemokines, nitric oxide—and the cytokine tornado funnel rips through the walls of blood vessels. And still the snakes replicate. Blood seeps throughout the bag of the body, bacteria wash out of their areas of containment, edema drowns the organs, sepsis triggers shock; it is suicide. And still the snakes replicate.

The spirits of our ancestors, routed by this plague, pour forth from their channels in the body like indignant fog, and chastise: O dreamers! The red earth herself is the body! The virus is we all of us!

Thus we all of us dreamed in the REM cycle before we woke to sit down to die.

The sun rose, and the solar light tower shut its lamps. The cook set mangoes in the canteen, but he had no motivation to make porridge. He, too, sat under the eaves, and we none of us ate. There was nothing to do but wait.

The delegation was coming today. For ten days, the camp director had bargained and pleaded and lied. He had rerouted our transport units and rescheduled our helicopter drops. He had run in-and-out of the ward to craft a statement from our doctor. He had called Geneva. He had called New York City. He had tasked we all of us to share his regular duties, while he fought like a cornered warthog to keep the delegation away.

We are a quarantine camp for patients with the plague of hemorrhagic fever. Isolation is our boon. For what do we need a lab? Why must we clear the protection of the surrounding bush to make way for more buildings—the living quarters for the scientists? Their recreation center? Their parking lot? More people is more waste, more pollution burden for the bush. More people need more water. Shall we run our aquifer dry? What water for the epidemic patients? A centrifuge, an autoclave, a cold chain require a generator, which needs petrol. Already our medicines and medical inventory must be dropped from helicopters to reach us in the bush. How so may petrol be supplied? All this development threatens the goals of quarantine. What will happen if these scientists fall ill?

And, of course, we object to the lying. We all of us are well-intentioned and hard working. We dwell here in the camp, on this periphery, and sacrifice that others may heal, that society may be free from an epidemic in its midst. The injury of underpayment for our labour is one we bear. The insult of lying we reject.

They told us it was a vaccine lab. We

have had prior collaboration with vaccine scientists. We know their operations. They work transparently. They do not seek isolation. They need no regular supply of epidemic patients for experiment. They do not undermine quarantine. The camp director welcomes honest researchers.

He fought this delegation because it is military. Its mission is to weaponize the virus. To make a weapon of a lethal virus for which there is no vaccine and no cure.

We all of us sat down to die. There is nothing to do but wait.

The sun was high when the delegation arrived. A delegation of foreigners to our camp is a noteworthy event. And we all of us do not take sides. Neutrality is our creed. But we were too sick to be neutral. We none of us received them at the gate.

The sounds of their vehicles and voices made their way to our ears. By their noise, we traced their path past triage, the ward, and the baobab tree that rises above it; past the borehole and the hand-pump; past the camp director's office, utility shed, facilities storeroom, garage, and the graveyard beyond them; past the canteen. When they arrived at the living quarters, they stopped. They stared at us, silent.

There they stood, tall, rigid, and gleaming. They gleamed with metal and with sweat. Their jaws were set, their eyes hidden behind black glasses. They were eighteen in their delegation, some many of them in uniform. They had traveled a long way, but they were ready, hungry for their work.

And we all of us reflected back to them the lassitude of those awaiting death.

After some minutes of this standoff, their readiness ebbed to confusion. We none of us met their black glasses or made motion to rise, until the camp director stirred from his fetal curl. With a heave, he lifted himself to sitting and then hoisted himself to stand. Our camp director is a man of dignity. His customary dress is a button-down shirt and slacks. Now, when he stood, he wore the t-shirt and shorts in which he had slept; his shoes were plastic slip-ons.

But his authority is internal. It is his spine. Even in the condition of group depression, our camp director stood before the delegation as a man of great authority.

They watched him like predatory birds. Then one of them said, "Is it *siesta*?"

We all of us speak at least three languages, but for none of us is English our first. This thing the man said we none of us understood. But this lack of comprehension was no dissuasion: "My friends," the camp director replied, "please. Accept my apologies. Come. I will show you first to the canteen. Come." He walked like a man carting his spirit behind him. "Have lunch. Drink some water." He offered his hand to the man who had spoken. The man's indifference was such that he accepted the handshake, and the camp director gestured that the delegation should follow. The men turned abruptly, their feet guided like by mechanical pivots.

As they walked away, the cook raised himself and trudged after the delegation to the canteen.

Today, we all of us make efforts to live.

For three days after the delegation came to take its measurements and conduct its assessments, we all of us continued to suffer the group depression. That third night, I sat on the packed red earth under the eaves the whole of the night, so bogged was my heart that I was mired in place.

In the darkest hour on that third night, an aardvark showed itself. It trundled past, head down, snout snuffling the ground, its rabbit ears rotating like antennae. Despite my melancholia, I felt an opening, an interest: dear digger! Perfect creature. Solitary, the aardvark knows no loneliness. Its skin is impenetrable to termite bites; its ears are sensitive to a leopard paw-step beyond the range of sight. It emits no scent but the dirt that coats it. Each night it digs to eat the insects of the earth, sleeps in the burrow of its own creation, and the next night, digs again. By its work, it contributes shelter for the many ground-dwelling animals of the bush: hyena, porcupine, snake, warthog. The aardvark is the foundation animal for the fauna ecology of the bush. As I myself know that termite mounds are scarce at this camp, this aardvark must travel farther still for its meal; its passage through here is simple grace. A reminder that the foundation is composed of the small and well-purposed.

On the fourth day, the ward director developed symptoms of hemorrhagic fever. His in-and-out of the ward to compose the written statement with the doctor seems to have been the mode of exposure. He did not touch the patients, and the doctor herself left the ward to converse with him, but in his haste and anxiety he had been neglectful. He had not worn the gown, facemask, and gloves that are required isolation precautions. The doctor had reprimanded him, and he had agreed with her that he must follow procedures. For what he did, he would have had to fire one of his staff. For himself, the consequences were plague.

He infected also the head of security, the pharmacy manager, and the cook during his period of incubation. The ward manager, medical techs, and triage tech, by virtue of their jobs, were wearing isolation precautions in their interactions with him, and so escaped infection. I myself am a survivor of this epidemic. I am immune.

As there is no camp, no place of safety, no space of healing, without we all of us—we all of us alive, and the spirits of our ancestors, together—we all of us today make efforts to live. The ward manager is doing most of the camp manager's work, and I am helping with the ward manager's job.

I am only the logistics manager, but on the ward, I supervise the medical techs and minister to the patients. I change the IV bags that hydrate the patients, and I prepare the narcotics injections for the doctor to administer.

The camp director, cook, pharmacy manager, and head of security know they are lucky. They are receiving treatment immediate upon presentation of symptoms. And our doctor has treated the virus with such wisdom that not one of our patients has succumbed yet to death. We all of us make efforts to live, but we none of us are waiting to die. When the camp director is lucid and his fever subsides, he blames himself for infecting the others. He complains of taking a bed from a patient who needs it.

The cook murmurs in his mother tongue of his longing for his family, his children whom he misses, his grandmother who died.

The pharmacy manager makes jokes at my expense about the upcoming narcotics audit.

And the head of security sings the praises of the camp director. "They'll not return now, those vaccinators," he says, the smile wide on his face even as his gums leak blood. Tears run from his eyes, but they are of laughter; it hurts him to laugh. "The virus supply they can harvest now from their own bodies."

If I love myself, does fame matter?

ANN NONI MINI

Across the Sudd, the animals are migrating—white-eared kob, antelope, gazelle—and so, too, the plague moves in its cycle. From its reservoir, the virus broke out to kill many and leave some few of us survivors immune, and now its tide of death recedes. The government declares the epidemic at an end. No more do quarantine transports deliver to us new patients. Our doctor deems all our patients recovered. And we all of us are ordered to shutter our quarantine camp.

Our narcotics are audited, our medical supplies are crated, our equipment is loaded onto trucks. Emptying of septic tanks is accomplished. Waste is burned. Measures to preserve the borehole and well are implemented. Our people are dispersed. Our camp director and pharmacy manager are in Juba, in conference with our colleagues at the country headquarters of our organization. Our head of security is overseeing the safe transport of our inventory. Our doctor is treating patients at her new assignment.

I have some small tasks to complete before I join the diaspora. The ward is empty except for sunlight. I am crossing the room when a medical tech, clad in street clothes— so different from the isolation precautions of gown, facemask and gloves!—enters with a broom and dustpan. The sound of bristles against the floor is loud. The sound of my flip-flops slapping my soles is loud. The sound of laughter from the pediatric ward is loud.

I stand in the doorway of the pediatric ward. The triage tech, also in street clothes, is laughing and clapping. Another medical tech, the one we all of us call, "Angel," is smiling widely. The focus of their attention is a little girl performing cartwheels.

Our last patient. Our lost patient.

Ann Noni Mini. Christian name. Tribal name. Pet name.

She came to us without family or papers. We think she is perhaps five. We assume her entire family is dead. She arrived limp as a swath of linen cloth and so hot to the touch. Blood fever made her first insensible, then wiped away her memory. When a person holding her medical chart asks her name, she say, "Ann." Ann only. She squints, thoughtful, when pressed for her family name.

Where do you live? Are your parents alive? What languages do you speak? Is English your first language? Have you been to school? Are you a Christian? To all these questions, she squints.

When her hemorrhagic fever subsides, she runs around the pediatric ward. So happy, so vitalized! She is unbothered being without family, tribe, nation; without information about who she is.

The triage tech takes her outside to teach her the names and properties of the plants. To give her something to remember. He says, "The baobab tree is the world's largest succulent plant, Ann," and she replies, "Uncle. Call Ann 'Noni.'"

We all of us scrutinized this clue. Is "Noni" short for "Muthoni"? Are you Kikuyu? Is your family from Kenya? She squints in reply.

With no one to take her, the camp director enrolls her in boarding school. He registers her giving his last name for her own. I know he pays her school fees himself.

While Noni remains at the camp before the session start, Angel is tasked with schooling her. Noni with a book in her hands is overjoyed. Before they open it, Angel asks, "What letter is first in, 'Noni'?" "Auntie, you call me, 'Mini'!" the child directs, laughing and opening the book to a page featuring an aardvark beside the letter, "A." "Mini starts with 'M'!"

A little angel.

"Noni," I say to her now, "Cook has made you pudding. Go and eat it, so he can close the kitchen." I look at Angel and the triage tech. "There is boxed lunch for us for the road." They nod.

While Angel and the triage tech take Noni to the canteen, I retrieve a shovel from the utilities shed and walk out to the grave-yard beyond the garage. Seventeen graves there are, all unmarked. We did not know their names. They were ambushers: men who lay in wait for the convoys delivering our supplies. They died of fright the night the convoy brought our doctor. Their bod-ies were carted to us, along with the lone survivor, the one of their number who told us their tale, and then, once here, and penitent, trained to be our triage tech. His hand that once raised weapons to hurt us now guides Noni to the canteen for pudding.

Seventeen graves. And one furrow. This furrow resulted from the trench collapse of a grave I dug. A visitor to our camp, a European, a grieving man, had asked me to dig the grave. I shake my head remembering him. "Some things can be explained," he had said. But many things remain unknowable.

I had covered the furrow and surrounding piles of earth with a tarp, secured in place with bricks. Now that we know we would not bury another, the camp director tasked me to refill this grave completely.

I stack the bricks. I fold the tarp. The redness of the earth in the scoop of my shovel gleams in the sunlight. It is the wrong time of day for this work. Too hot. Sweat soaks me before I have begun. But, by tea-time, I too must vacate this camp for my next assignment. So, in the heat of the day, I dig.

"Uncle, what are you doing?"

Noni circles me, running with her arms held out, like she is an aeroplane. She is smiling and energetic with sugar, stickiness glinting around her mouth.

I straighten my back, grateful for the break, and wipe sweat out of my eyes. "Uncle is filling a grave."

"Whose grave?" she sing-songs.

I shake my head. "I dug this grave for an unknown person."

"Then it is my grave." She stops. She looks up at me with earnest eyes.

I am taken with surprise. It rips me from my body. I completely forget that I am drenched in sweat. In fact, I feel breeze on my cheekbones and armpits. I notice the thickness that arose in my throat only after. "What?"

"Ann-Noni-Mini—unknown person is my name," she laughs, her eyes sparkling.

Could such a young child make such a clever pun? I am uncomfortable, unsure if I am in the presence of something uncommon. A big thing working through a little person, like a miracle. "You are not anonymous," I say with an uncertain smile.

"No, a mouse is small. I am even more mini." Her face is without self-pity. She is simply sincere.

"This grave is not for you," I say quietly, urgently.

"Uncle," she corrects me, "it is the only thing that is mine." She is so excited to have something of her own.

I kneel now, so that her brown eyes may be on direct level with my pupils. "Noni," I ask, "will you let Uncle fill this grave? If you need it later, Friend Aardvark will dig it again for you. Is that ok?"

She nods seriously. Then she giggles ebulliently.

"Miiiinnniii!" calls Angel from the distance of the canteen. I can see the box lunch in Angel's hands, ready for the *matutu* ride to Juba, the next stop before everything else—Angel's next assignment, Noni's schooling.

Noni smiles at me, claps her hands, and runs away.

I return to my task.

I will obliterate all trace of this grave. Make smooth the earth so no possibility exists that this gravesite may be found again.

It is not three shovelfuls of earth, though, before I feel the fear. My arms are trembling. I grip the shovel with frustration. She is safe and getting an education, and nothing in my material conditions has changed. What should I fear?

But Noni's words make me feel I have brushed against the unfathomable.

I comfort myself with a thought: it is just the end. Endings are frightening. Even happy endings contain the terrifying seed of the unknown next.

When I next saw the camp director, it was some many months later. Our organization had sent me to the refugee camp in Jonglei, him to the camp in Doro, for our next assignments, but I obtained leave when he called.

He had gone to the boarding school to claim her body. Her school records somehow included a note about her "ownership" of a grave plot at the old quarantine campsite: her land, the only place that was hers. When he saw the note, the camp director knew it was right to bury her there, where we all of us had found her, among others of the unknowns. Would I, he asked me on the phone, re-dig the grave?

I had told her I would do so. It was right to keep my word.

The boarding school had declined to furnish the students with mosquito nets for their beds. She had contracted dengue fever. Coming so soon after her bout of hemorrhagic fever, the dengue virus was fatal.

We both of us stood together at the edge of the grave looking down at the body bag. It was too small and limp as a swath of linen cloth against the red earth.

I was glad of the shovel now. Its handle was a tiller with which I could navigate these next moments. I bury her.

Shoveling dirt is a physical act that requires no thought and no feeling. It is satisfying exertion at a time when no effort can be of avail—satisfying because it is not effort, but acceptance.

"We have no stone," the camp director said heavily. Then he became agitated. "After the indignity of a life with no name, no family, she cannot be left with no grave marker!"

I pause, securing the shovelhead in a pile of earth, and look at him.

"How will anyone know she existed?" he asks, anguished.

I reach out my arm and hold tightly to his shoulder. "There is no indignity in truth," I say.

I think he understands. He calms.

I return to burial. Whether anyone knows she existed does not matter. Whether she actually existed does not matter. Her function was so basic; many waste their overcomplicated lives in hopeless pursuit of her effortless success. Now she is a story the camp director will recount, a story I will tell, Angel will tell, we all of us tell; and it matters not if she was always a story and never a little girl at all. Ann Noni Mini, like we all of us, was a structure to conduct love. A conduit. She arose out of love, stayed for some time, giving and receiving love, and then dissipated, scattering her love to be conducted through some other conduit.

This is truth. She embraced it. In that, there is only dignity.

Acknowledgements

Five of the six stories in *The Plague Cycle* have been published previously in the following literary journals:

"The Body and the Virus" in *Gone Lawn*; "The Sudd" in *Thrice*; "Tourist in Hades" in *Loud Zoo*; "Ann Noni Mini" in *Dime Show Review*; and "To the Depths" in *The Missing Slate*.

I am especially grateful to Madison Smartt Bell, Tod Thilleman, Jackson Willis, Nathanael Absher, Elias Ohrstrom, Katie Feild, Kate Wyer, Peter Dayton, Aaron Thacker, Vicki Schassler, Julian Fernandez, Brendan Jines, India Lamb, Dara Crawley, Madeline St. John, Swade Best, Alyssa Krasnansky, and S.N. Goenka.